Move Over!

By Janine Amos and Annabel Spenceley
Consultant Rachael Underwood

CHERRYTREE BOOKS

A CHERRYTREE BOOK

This edition first published in 2007
by Cherrytree Books, part of
The Evans Publishing Group
2A Portman Mansions
Chiltern Street
London
W1U 6NR

© Evans Brothers Limited 2007

Printed in China

British Library Cataloguing in Publication Data.

Amos, Janine
  Move over!. - (Good friends)
  1. Personal space - Pictorial works - Juvenile fiction
  2. Children's stories - Pictorial works
  I. Title II. Spenceley, Annabel III. Underwood, Rachael
  823.9'14[J]

ISBN: 1842344315
13 digit ISBN 978 1842344316

CREDITS
Editor: Louise John
Designer: D.R.ink
Photography: Gareth Boden
Production: Jenny Mulvanny
Based on the original edition of Move Over! published in 1999

With thanks to our models:
The tent
Amelia John, Elizabeth Walsingham, Grace Walsingham,
Charley Winter, Sophie Gleghorn and Alistair Gleghorn.
The rocket
Callum Palmer, Carl Robertson and Luke Reynolds.

VISIT OUR WEBSITE
www.evansbooks.co.uk
Evans

The Tent

Amelia is playing in the tent.

Here comes Elizabeth.

Amelia and Elizabeth are in the tent.

Here come Grace and Charley.

Amelia, Elizabeth, Grace and Charley are all in the tent.

Here comes Sophie.

Sophie squeezes into the tent.

How do the others feel?

"Move over!"
grumbles Charley.
"I'm squashed."

11

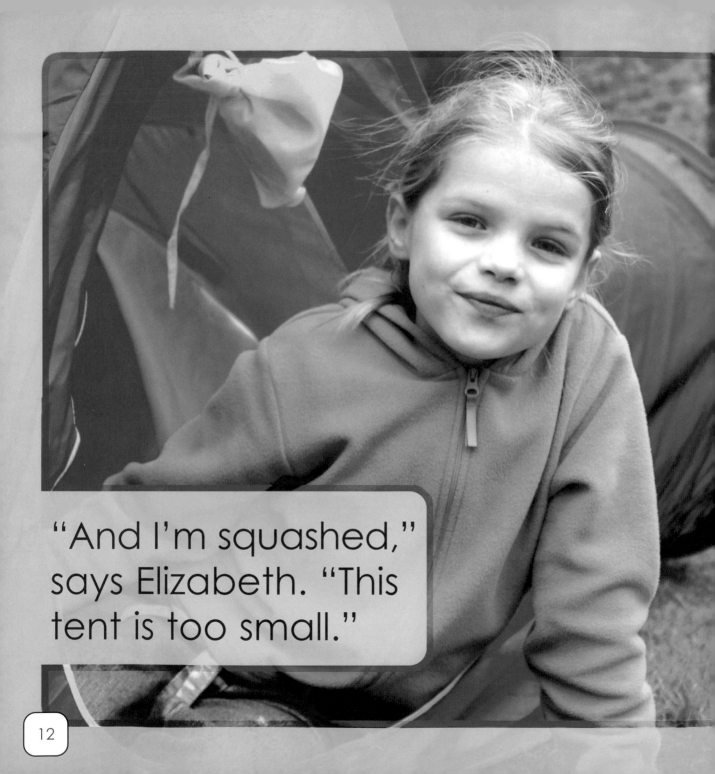

"And I'm squashed," says Elizabeth. "This tent is too small."

Elizabeth crawls out.

Elizabeth gets two chairs.

"I need this rug," she says.
"Help me, Sophie."

Elizabeth and Sophie
make another tent.

Now there's room
for everyone.

Oh dear!
Here comes Alistair.

The Rocket

The table is covered with boxes. Callum is building a rocket.

"Hey! Move Over! I need more space," says Carl.

"Zoom! Zoom!"
goes Callum.

"Move over!" shouts Carl. He pushes the boxes on to the floor.

"What's going on here?" asks Luke. "You two look upset."

"Carl pushed my boxes," says Callum.

"He's taking up all the table. There's no room for me," says Carl.

"So you both need more space," says Luke. "What can we do?"

"I've got a good idea," says Callum. "I could build my rocket upwards."

"Show me!" says Luke. Callum holds his rocket up.

"Look! There's space for me now!" smiles Carl.

Callum finishes his rocket.
And Carl makes his space buggy.

TEACHER'S NOTES

By reading these books with young children and inviting them to answer the questions posed in the text the children can actively work towards aspects of the PSHE and Citizenship curriculum.

Develop confidence and responsibility and making the most of their abilities by
- recognising what they like and dislike, what is fair and unfair and what is right and wrong
- to share their opinions on things that matter to them and explain their views
- to recognise, name and deal with their feelings in a positive way

Develop good relationships and respecting the differences between people
- to recognise how their behaviour affects others
- to listen to other people and play and work co-operatively
- to identify and respect the difference and similarities between people

By using some simple follow up and extension activities, children can also work towards

Citizenship KS1
- to recognise choices that they can make and recognise the difference between right and wrong
- to realise that people and living things have needs, and that they have a responsibility to meet them
- that family and friends should care for each other

EXTENSION ACTIVITY
Circle Time
- Seat the children in a circle. Read the first story in *Move Over!* and ask the children to contribute answers to the questions posed on page 10 of the text.
- Pass an object such as a toy or a stone around the circle. Only the person holding the object is allowed to speak. Ask the children to name one thing they like to do outdoors (camping, playgrounds, ride bikes, sports and so on).
- Going around the circle, turn pairs of children to face one another. Ask them to talk only to their partner. Remind the children of the story and ask them to discuss together the reasons why they think Charley and Elizabeth were getting fed-up in the tent. After a minute or so ask the children to turn around again and share their ideas with the group.
- Look at the last picture in the story. Ask the children to think about what might happen next? What could the children do to find room for Alistair?
- Then pass the object around the circle and ask the children to state one thing that they have done well during the Circle Time, such as listening, taking turns, talking to a partner, putting up their hand, sitting still, etc.

These activities can be repeated on subsequent days using the other story in the book or with other stories in the series.